Why Did We Have to Move Here?

Sally J. K. Davies

Carolrhoda Books, Inc. / Minneapolis

Cover calligraphy by Sally J. K. Davies

Text and illustrations copyright © 1997 by Sally J. K. Davies

Carolrhoda Books, Inc. c/o The Lerner Publishing Group
241 First Avenue North, Minneapolis, MN 55401 U.S.A.

Library of Congress Cataloging–in–Publication Data

Davies, Sally J. K.
  Why did we have to move here / by Sally J. K. Davies.
      p.   cm.
  Summary: A young boy has trouble adjusting to his new home and his
new school, until he decides that with a little effort, he can make new friends.
  ISBN 1-57505-046-3
  [1. Moving, Household–Fiction. 2. Schools–Fiction.
3. Friendship–Fiction.] I. Title.
PZ7.D284445Wh   1997
[E]–dc21   96-44995

Manufactured in the United States of America
1 2 3 4 5 6 – JR – 02 01 00 99 98 97

This book is dedicated to

all my old friends in Canada,

whom I miss very much,

and all my new friends

in the United States of America,

who gave me such a wonderful welcome.

S. J. K. D.

My dinosaur tail broke off in the moving van
and when I finally found the box with the glue in
it the bottle had exploded all over my favorite
books, and I can't remember where I packed my
Saturn night-light, but Mum said don't worry
because at this house I'll be sharing a bedroom
with my brother.

Why did we have to move here?

This would never have
happened at the other house.
I had a room of my own
at the other house, and
I have never heard
anyone snore
so loud.

Why did we have to move?

It was icy and rainy when Mum took me to my new school, and I had to wear my ugly old winter coat because my raincoat was still packed away somewhere and my stupid boots leaked, and when I got to the classroom everyone stared at me.

I miss my old school. I wonder if my friends miss me.

The teacher gave me the only empty desk, which was right near the loud, grinding pencil sharpener, and I couldn't see over the big head in front of me, and when I raised my hand to ask to go to the bathroom the teacher didn't notice me until it was almost too late.

This would never have happened at my old school.

Everyone formed groups to
work on their science projects, and
when the teacher asked if anyone
would like me to join their group
no one answered so she made
me work with the twins.

I always had a great partner in my old class.

In art class we all drew weird monsters, and the teacher put a girl's drawing on the front display board and everyone said it was the scariest monster they'd ever seen and that she was the best artist in the class.

I thought my drawing was pretty good too. At my old school everyone loved my monster-lizard drawings.

I want to go back where they like me.

When I opened my math book it all looked so different, and when the teacher said we'd be having a big test tomorrow I felt sick. We never learned this stuff at my old school.

I used to love math, but I'm not so sure anymore.

It rained all day and when they announced an indoor recess the teacher asked Peter to give me a tour of the school, but as soon as the bell rang he ran over to play with Nikhil and Jess and I guess he forgot about me.

Well, I have friends too . . .

at my old school.

Everyone whispered and giggled and joked

with their friends and I felt foolish and out of

place, but I didn't want to stand there all by myself

and Peter had promised

to show me around.

So I took a deep breath. And
I made myself go over to Peter and
the others.

When I smiled and said
hello, Peter told me I had
a funny accent. I told *him*
that *he* was the one who
talked funny. He just
grinned and asked me to say
something else.

I had a really smart
answer to that.
But it took all
my courage to
say it out loud.

"Something else!" I shouted back,

and they all laughed with me.

After school it stopped raining, but the ground
and trees were thick with ice. All the kids slid
along the sidewalks, screaming and shouting with
their friends, and I heard Jess tell Peter and Nikhil
to bring their ice skates down to the pond. But
they didn't ask me to go with them.

I remembered the lake at my old park. In winter we'd fly over the ice on our skates and race with the wind. The pond here was small, but I was sure there was room for me too. I decided to go. I'd show them how fast and strong I could skate.

I finally discovered my skates
in a box marked Laundry Room:
Miscellaneous Fragile. I raced
down to the pond, past the tennis
courts and swings. But I arrived
just in time to hear a big lady
scream, "Stop! Can't you see?
This ice is not safe!"

NO SKATING
NO BOATING
NO SWIMMING

"It just isn't fair!" I wanted to yell. Everyone

looked as upset as I felt.

Then an idea popped right into my head.

I called out to them all, "Hey, follow me! There's great ice over here. It's thick and it's flat and it's perfect for us!"

At the old park I never thought of skating on a

tennis court!

But there are lots of new things that I'd

never have done if we hadn't moved here.

I guess all my old friends were once

new friends. . . .

So maybe I'll stay here awhile.

How This Story Came to Be

When I was in first grade, my family moved to Calgary, in western Canada. I was born in England and my parents are British, so I probably sounded strange to my new Canadian classmates. They teased me.

Once, my teacher marked an answer on a test wrong because I called a baby carriage a pram. They both mean the same thing but my teacher had never heard a baby carriage called a pram. I had never heard a pram called a baby carriage!

Three years later, my family moved to Ottawa, Ontario, in the middle of the school year. It seemed like everyone at my new school had a best friend, except me. I was also disappointed to learn that another student was considered the "best-artist-in-the-class." At my old school, everyone loved my drawings.

I've moved many times since then. Each time I arrive in a new place, it takes a little while but I always discover wonderful new friends.

The first winter after I moved to Maryland, we had several big ice storms. So guess what I did? I went skating on a tennis court, of course, with my very best friend, Derrick. And that is how this story came to be.

Sally

TENNIS COURT RULES

1. Play begins on the hour.
2. Bikes, skateboards, and roller skates are prohibited within the court area.
3. Food, beverages, and glass are prohibited within court area.
4. Tennis lessons and tournaments are permited only with a permit.

PARK POLICE